Nathaniel Clame 4/96   1.30

OLD JAKE
and the
PIRATE'S TREASURE

OLD JAKE

and the

PIRATE'S TREASURE

By BETTY HAGER

Drawings by RON DAWKINS

Harvey House, Publishers
New York City, New York

Manufactured in the United States of America

ISBN 0-8178-0006-9
Library of Congress Card Catalog No. 80-80606

Harvey House, Publishers
20 Waterside Plaza, New York, N.Y. 10010

Published in Canada by Fitzhenry & Whiteside, Ltd., Toronto

For all the Children I have known at
Shepherd of the Valley Elementary
School in Canoga Park.

TABLE OF CONTENTS

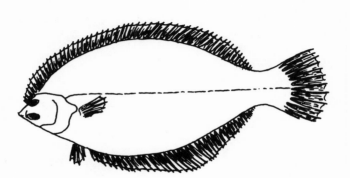

Chapter One

Old Jake's House

I believe my big brother, Raymie, and I, along with his friend Hank Thompson, were the only people who ever went into Old Jake Brusarde's home.

I know we did wrong to do it. It was trespassing, and that's a crime. I suppose we were curious because of all the strange tales we heard about him. He was a Cajun from Louisiana who had only lived in Bayou La Batre for about four years. He did some peculiar things that made us all wonder. Once he drove his car in to Mobile, forgot it, and hitch hiked the thirty miles back home to Bayou La Batre.

The thing that really made us curious was the treasure. He hadn't found one, but people said he owned a treasure map from one of Jean Laffite's sunken pirate ships. That ship ws said to have had valuable jewels and coins on it, and a person who had one of these maps could very likely be rich one day.

I happened to go along with Hank and Raymie because of the flounders. Those are fish with flat bodies.

They lie along the sandy waters of the bay. You catch them at night by going out with a lantern and a gig. Papa said Raymie was too young to flounder alone, because the gig was dangerous.

Anyhow, my brother and his friend decided they were going to explore Old Jake's house. They never would have taken me along, but I knew they were sneaking out after midnight to go floundering, and I told them I'd tell Papa if they didn't let me go.

Raymie didn't want Papa to know his secret, so he promised to let me go along when they explored Old Jake's home. I was ashamed of tricking him that way, so I shoved my concience way back in a corner of my mind. I let myself think of the exciting thing that was going to happen to me.

One day, in the last week of May, Raymie asked Papa if he could get off work early. He worked after school for Papa in our Marine, Hardware, and Supply Store. It was right on the water, across the street from my house.

"Could Hank and I borrow the skiff?"

"What are you fellows up to?" Papa asked.

"Oh, we have something we want to see down at the head of the bayou." Raymie never did lie outright to Papa, but he was a little secretive at times. I think he never did fool Papa, though.

When Papa didn't answer right away, he said, "We'll take Marcie along."

10

I guess Papa thought they couldn't be doing anything too wild if they were willing to take a little eight year old girl with them.

"Alright, but don't stay too late, and take good care of your little sister," he said.

We shoved off from the wharf of the hardware store at six o'clock. Raymie and Hank rowed up to the head of the bayou to Snake Creek and tied the skiff at Skinner's Landing.

"Now, Marcie, you crouch down low in the marsh. I'll squash you flatter than a flounder if you let anyone see or hear you!" he threatened.

"Stop being so bossy!" I said. I hated being eight years old.

Sometimes Hank acted like he thought he was my brother, too, and believe me, one brother is enough! He pushed that red hair off his forehead and stared at me with those light blue eyes.

"I'll help flatten you," he said. "Now just follow us, and hide behind those old oaks leading up to the house."

We slipped from tree to tree. I had never done such a sneaky thing before. I kept wondering what would happen if we were caught. I wished that it was darker. Raymie made a big circle around the house to be certain Old Jake wasn't home.

I think we were all surprised when we saw the house. It wasn't as large as we expected. Even though there were two floors there seemed to be only one or two rooms on each floor. It looked as if the whole skinny thing would fall if it weren't for the tree.

It was a large, sprawling oak. One big branch brushed close to a narrow, upstairs window. The window was open, and a yellowed curtain blew outside. It looked like ghosts' arms, inviting us in.

The grey moss, clinging thickly to the branches, got in our way, but we shoved it aside. I shinnied up first, because I was the smallest. Crawling through that narrow window wasn't easy for them, but after a little tugging, the three of us were in Old Jake's bedroom.

The room was small. In one corner was a tousled bed. Next to it was a table with a kerosene lamp. There were no rugs on the floor. The planks had some spaces between them, and we could see glints of light from below.

A door slammed downstairs.

"Oh gosh. Now we're going to be caught for sure!" I said in a whispered wail.

Raymie slapped a hand over my mouth. I pushed him away and scrambled for the window. Raymie and Hank blocked my exit.

Old Jake was underneath the tree!

Quickly we pulled back and flattened ourselves against the wall, breathing hard.

"He wasn't down here when we came in, was he?" Raymie whispered.

"Nah, he wasn't," I said.

"How are we gonna get outa here?" Hank asked.

"Let's just go down the stairs, and maybe we can slip out the back door." I said.

"I knew we should have left you at home, Shrimp," Raymie said.

"Yeah," Hank agreed.

I stuck my tongue out at them.

"While we're here, why don't we see if the map is here?" Raymie suggested.

"If he catches us, he might think we're stealing it," I said.

Hank lifted the mattress. There wasn't anything under it. For a few minutes they searched the room. I stood by the stairwell, nervously peering down. They found only a few shirts and pants hanging sloppily. A greasy brown hat sagged limply from a hook.

There was a sudden clumping noise downstairs.

"Let's get out of here!" Hank said. I was weak-kneed with fear, but I had to smile at Big Shot fourteen-year-old Hank; he was as scared as I was.

We heard the door and figured he had gone outside again.

"Maybe you're right, Marcie, let's try the stairs," Raymie said.

The stairs were narrow boards which angled steeply to the first floor. We tried to walk softly on them, but they creeked noisily. We were half way down when it happened. One of the boards was out, and when I stumbled the noise was terrible.

"Oh, no," I groaned.

A kerosene lamp was held high, and the rays landed full blast on Raymie, Hank and me!

Behind the lamp was the errie form of Old Jake. His face was like his house. The hair was coarse and grey like the Spanish moss on the oak outside. His eyes were small and black, peering from dark caverns above his cheekbones. A sunken, toothless mouth scowled under a hooked nose.

"What you do in my house? You steal from Old Jake, hah?"

When Hank didn't answer, Raymie tried, but his voice squeaked when it came out.

"We just . . . Oh, sir, we didn't . . . I mean, we wouldn't *take* nothin'. We were just curious!" he said.

"Coo-rus!?" Old Jake shreiked. "You come down dem stairs! I teach you what happen to coo-rus thieves what come to sneak 'round my house! Go into de kitchen!"

We went. I was surprised to feel Raymie's hand on my shoulder, sort of protecting me. Maybe he liked me, after all.

Old Jake's eyes cut into us. We could feel them.

He shoved us into unsteady chairs. We should have

14

felt better sitting down, but what we saw on the table didn't help any. There were two knives. One was a dull little oyster knife. The other was a sharp, red-handled butcher knife.

I wanted to cry, but for some strange reason, Raymie's comforting hand made me try to be brave.

I saw Raymie lift his other hand from his lap. I knew he planned to take the knife, but Old Jake was too fast for him! In a breath his rough hand grasped that red handle.

His hands were horrible because of the fingernails. They were stained yellow, and they curved back to his palms like those of a demon.

He stood behind us with a knife first at Raymie's neck and then at Hank's. He didn't touch me. It's a good thing he didn't. I know I would have died right there at that rickety table.

"You, you empty de pockets!" he snarled hoarsely.

The boys did. When Jake saw only string, fish hooks, and a few pennies, he screeched, "Where you hide it?"

"We didn't hide nothin'. Honest," Hank said. His voice came out as squeaky as Raymie's had.

"Yeah, honest," I said softly, but I don't think anyone heard me.

Jake began to circle us. His body was bent almost double, and he held the knife behind his back.

The only sounds were Jake's heavy breathing and the crickets singing in the marsh. Hearing the crickets made me realize that twilight was turning into night.

In a lightning movement Old Jake rushed to the table. I knew we were going to die now.

But a strange thing happened. He began to sputter, and cackle, and screech. We couldn't believe it, but he was laughing.

"Go! Gat out!"

We didn't move. We weren't sure he meant it.

"You hear me? You leave!"

I don't remember getting into the skiff, but it was dusk as we rowed back up the bayou.

Raymie began to laugh. I thought for a while that he was crying. He doubled over the oars, and there were tears in his eyes.

"I swear that was the best time I ever had."

"Yeah . . ." Hank choked, holding his sides.

They were both laughing hard now, but somehow I could tell neither one really thought anything was funny. I knew we were all glad to get out of there. Something else, too. No one said anything, but I could tell we all felt ashamed that we had trespassed on that old man's property. There was a feeling of relief that we had gotten away without something serious happening to us.

We were late for supper, but Mama and Papa didn't say much. Raymie and I ate our shrimp gumbo quietly, and even Raymie was glad to go to bed early.

Chapter Two

The Mysterious Fire

Our school ended on May 31st that year. It's hot in Alabama, and the schools let out early.

There were only 300 children in the entire school, from the first to the eleventh grades. All our classrooms were in the same two storied building. The school was almost two miles from my house.

All year I met Jeanne' where the sidewalk began along the highway, and we walked to school together.

Jeanne' was part French, like most of the people in my town. I couldn't understand why her hair and eyes weren't black like mine. I thought she was beautiful because she was a towhead, and her eyes were big and blue. Her front teeth protruded a little, and this gave her a special look. She had freckles all over her face, arms, and legs. I wanted to have freckles instead of getting dark in the summer. Jeanne' and I tried to bleach me out once, with corn meal and milk, but it didn't work. She said next time we'd use Arm and Hammer baking soda.

Jeanne' said she thought I could be a movie star. She

liked black hair and eyes the way I liked blond hair and blue eyes. I didn't think I was pretty. I felt bad because I was shrimpy. Well, that's what Hank and Raymie said. Jeanne' was tall for her age, and no one ever called her a shrimp.

Also, I kept asking Mama to let me grow my hair out, but Mama said the Buster Brown hair cut was "in style" for girls in 1932 and easy to care for.

Well, Jeanne' and I weren't a bit alike in the way we looked, but we liked the same things. Jeanne' was a pretender like I was. Together we knew how to make dreams happen.

We especially liked the summers. We'd hike around the coast to swim in the shallow, warm waters of the bay. We could walk out a mile before the water was over our heads, so Mama didn't worry about us much. We would be mermaids or Moses' mother and Pharoah's daughter.

At the icy creek, we'd swing from a rope tied to a big oak that branched out over the water. We'd pretend we were Jean Lafitte and his men, pirating a ship.

Sometimes we'd gather scoop nets, fat meat bait, and string and go crabbing over at Delcambre's Wharf. If we got the crabs home before they died, Mama would boil them in a big, black pot in the back yard. We'd eat the sweet crab meat afterwards with ketsup and Louisiana hot sauce.

Sometimes Papa and Mama would invite Jeanne' to go to the picture show with us at Jardin's Movie House. It was a big tin and wood building on stilts over the bayou.

If we got there early, before the crowds came, we could hear the "pullip-pullip" of the water washing on the shore beneath us. Jeanne' and I loved the Shirley Temple movies, but Mama and Papa like Will Rogers.

Raymie had made me cross my heart and hope to die that I would never tell anyone about going to Old Jake's house. I never would have, either, if it hadn't been for a couple of things that happened in the next few week.

We had a revival in the First Baptist Church where my family goes to worship. I went forward at one of the meetings to confess my sins. The next Sunday I was baptised in Willow Creek with twenty other people.

Jeanne' said, in the Catholic Church where she goes, the nun said you should never lie again once you knew the catechism, 'cause then you know better. We made a special vow to each other that we never would lie, or keep a secret from each other, which was the same thing.

I got a needle and made a tiny scratch on my finger, and she made one on hers, too. We held our fingers together and promised that we were blood sisters and would never lie to each other again.

I didn't tell her my secret until later, though. I had a problem. To Raymie I had crossed my heart and hoped to die that I wouldn't tell, so I wasn't sure which promise I should keep.

On the last day of school something happened which made it all right for me to tell her. We were walking home from school together. It was hot and sticky, but we didn't mind. School was out!

"Why don't we ask our folks if we can go for a swim in the creek?" I asked Jeanne'.

"They wouldn't let us go alone." Jeanne' said.

"Well, we could ask if Raymie could take us."

"There's Raymie and Hank behind us now," Jeanne' said.

Sure enough, Raymie and Hank Thompson were walking several yards behind us.

"Hey, Raymie!" I called, "when we get home will you see if Papa will let you take us over to Willow Creek for a swim?"

"Maybe," Raymie said, "but it's the beginning of the shrimping season, and I may not be able to leave the shop."

"Most of the boats won't 'oil up' until later, I betcha," I said. "Won't you just ask him, please, Raymie?"

Papa must have been in a good mood. He said we could go.

By four o'clock Hank, Jeanne', Raymie and I were all at the wharf of Papa's hardware store. I'd picked up a cold, baked yam on my way through the kitchen. I pinched the deep wine-colored skin in half to share with Jeanne'.

Papa and a friend were sitting on the wharf. They had a bucket of oysters, oyster knives, crackers and ketchup. They'd shuck the oyster shells open, splash the oysters with ketchup, then plop them into their mouths with a flick of the oyster knife. I never would see how Papa ate raw oysters. They didn't look dead yet.

"Papa," I called, "Mama's going to be real put out with you if you eat too many oysters! She's fixin' a whole mess of turnip greens, pot likker and corn bread for supper . . . not to mention rice pudding."

"Okay, honey," he laughed. I liked the way Papa's blue eyes twinkled in his ruddy face.

Jeanne' and I begged to row the skiff, but we didn't reckon how heavy Raymie and Hank were. After struggling for a while, with the boys laughing at us, we gave up. We sat on the seat in the stern with our towels wadded in our laps, giddy and jumpy with joy. This was going to be our first swim of the year.

Hank and Raymie teased each other about some new girl who had moved to Bayou La Batre from Biloxi. Hank said Raymie was hankering to know her.

"I ain't hankering to know her. You're the *hank*-ering one."

Then they laughed so hard they almost dropped the oars. After we went under Grande Pont and were ready to turn left under the weeping willows, Raymie suddenly backwatered his oars and stood up.

"Hey, Hank, look! Over toward Snake Creek! There's a fire! It looks like it might be a house burning."

"Aw, come on, Raymie, we wanna go swimming.

Let's don't go see a fire! Please," I said.

"Shut up, Marcie! It won't take long. We'll just go check out what is is," Raymie said.

"I'm going to tell Mama you said 'shut up' to me, and she'll have Papa take care of you good," I said. I hoped that would worry him, and he'd turn around and go back to Willow Creek.

Hank said, "Y'know, it looks like it's by Pee Wee Skinner's landing."

I forgot all about our swim, then. I looked from Hank to Raymie, and I could see they were excited, maybe even worried. They rowed faster now. They were hot and perspiring. Even though I wasn't rowing, I felt warm and tingly with excitement.

When we reached Pee Wee's we saw it *was* Old Jake's house. Ten or fifteen people had arrived there before us. The house and the old oak were red-orange flames and billows of smoke.

Someone said Pee Wee had climbed out on that big limb by the upstairs window to be sure Old Jake wasn't trapped in the bedroom. Pee Wee had gotten down just in time.

"Raymie," I said, "Those stairs were steep! Are they sure he wasn't trapped on the stairs?"

"No," Raymie answered. "Pee Wee said he looked."

We waited till dark, watching it burn. When dusk had settled over the bayou, only one little lick of blue flame continued to burn. Nat Dupont said it was Old Jake's heart.

Mr. Todd Johnson said he believed Old Jake had set fire to his house and walked away with his treasure map.

"We'd better get home!" Raymie said, noticing the sun reflecting pink across the creek now.

We sat quietly in the rowboat. There was only the rhythmic "puh-lash, puh-lash" as the oars sliced into the water.

When we docked at the wharf and began to cross the crushed shell road to my house, Jeanne' grabbed my arm.

"Marcie Delchamps! *What* narrow stairs? Marcie, you are keeping something from me, and that's the same as telling a lie! You're wicked! You've forgotten we're blood sisters."

I was relieved to tell her. I had wanted to tell her all along.

Since it was the beginning of summer Mama said Hank and Jeanne' could spend the night with us.

We sat on the front porch late that night, talking about Old Jake, his house, and the fire. I wouldn't have thought those fourteen-year-olds would have wanted to talk with us, but we had something in common now. Hank and Raymie didn't mention the girl from Biloxi once.

The boys sat on the swing at the end of the porch, and Jeanne' and I sat on the steps. Now and then the white hull of a shrimp boat would glide past the hardware store, following its path along the bayou. I loved to hear the deep, mournful blasts of their horns as they headed out to the bay and into the gulf.

There must have been a million crickets and bullfrogs in the marsh.

Suddenly we heard a rustle in the shrubbery behind the huge magnolia tree in our front yard. There was a whistling "swish" and something landed on the steps near my bare feet.

We all stood at once, and I reached down to see what it was, my heart pumping madly.

It was a long, red-handled butcher knife. There was no doubt in my mind where I had seen that knife!

The sharp blade of it pierced through an old treasure map.

Chapter Three

The Will-o'-the-Wisp (or Feu Follet)

For a few moments all of us were still with fear; we couldn't move. Then Raymie and Hank made a wild dash across the yard to see who had thrown the knife. It was useless. They could find no one. Jeanne' and I were glad they couldn't.

We finally spread the map across the porch, trying to see by the small lantern which hung by the door. The map was worn and torn at the creases, but even Jeanne' and I could tell it was an old map of Bayou La Batre. One entire corner had been torn away.

None of us could make any sense out of it. We all agreed it was the same red-handled butcher knife, but where was Old Jake? Why did he want us to have his treasure map, and why was a corner of the map missing?

A few weeks later another strange thing happened that made that summer one of the most exciting of my life.

We were sitting around the living room listening to "Amos and Andy" on the radio. I was snuggled on Papa's lap when I heard Hank come up the walk, yelling his head off for Raymie.

He never knocked. He came banging through the screened door, almost knocking the fan over that Mama had placed on the floor.

"Mr. Dudley! Mr. Dudley! Raymie! There's Will-o'-the-Wisp up to the head of the bayou! I seen it with my own eyes! I was catching tadpoles with Herbert Del-Rey, and it started coming at us as big as sin!"

Hank was pale, and his eyes were as big as oysters.

"We got outa there as fast as we could. I tell you, that old headless ghost almost got us! Do you wanna go back with us, Raymie?"

I jumped down from Papa's knee to listen better. It seemed odd to me that Hank would want to go back to see some headless thing that had almost gotten him.

"You oughta see all the cars and rowboats goin' over there. Why, you'd think all that commotion would scare that old fisherman's ghost away, but he's still floatin' all over that marsh, lookin' for his head."

"What head? What fisherman?" I asked, but no one was listening to me.

Raymie was saying, "Hey, Pop, can I use the skiff? I won't stay too late."

Still no one thought of me. Like I said before, I hated being eight years old. Mama and Papa let Raymie do anything.

)ulled at Mama's elbow.

Mama," I whispered, "Mama! What's a will-o'-the-
"

Mama said, "Honey, the Will-o'-the-Wisp is a legend, you know, an old wive's tale."

I didn't know, because I wasn't sure what an old wive's tale was. I'd heard about a legend at school, but I couldn't remember what I'd heard.

"But what *is* a will-o'-the-wisp?" I asked again.

Mama smiled that big, wide, smile of hers, the teasing one, and explained.

"In Louisiana they call that Feu Follet, or Crazy Fire. The Bayou La Batre legend says that there was once a fisherman who lived in a little shack in the marsh at the head of the bayou. He would get up early, light his lantern, and look for bait before going fishing in the bay.

"A famous pirate who had his headquarters on Grand Isle in Louisiana would often hide his pirate fleet in a cove at the mouth of the bayou. You've heard of him — Jean Lafitte?

"Well, one morning the pirates slipped into the creek, snatched away the fisherman's beautiful wife, and cut his head off."

Mama rolled her black eyes and laughed.

"The Will-o'-the-Wisp is supposed to be the blue lanern of the fisherman, searching for his head."

"Is that true?" I asked, knowing it wasn't, and half-hoping it was.

Mama laughed and said, "Of course not!"

Raymie and Hank were making plans to go down to Papa's store to get the oars for the skiff. They were loud with excitement. My heart was beating wildly. I knew that I had to be included.

"Please, Papa, let me go! Mama?"

I pleaded and coaxed until Raymie said, "Aw, let her go. We'll take care of her."

Raymie was afraid they'd have a change of heart and not even let him go.

Papa asked, "Will you watch after her carefully?"

And Raymie said, "Sure, Papa, we'll take care of the little shrimp."

He grabbed me by the hair and pulled me along. I squealed and giggled all the way across the shell road, up the rough planks of the wharf, and into the skiff. The smell of tar, oil, and fish was strong. Tonight it smelled like adventure.

I sat in the stern of the boat. Raymie and Hank sat in the middle and put the oars into the oarlocks. Together they cut the blades smoothly into the water.

They rowed past lines of shacks, wharves, shrimp factories and fishing boats. We slipped under Grande Pont, the big bridge which opened up when boats with tall masts went through. They rowed until we saw only an occasional glimmer of kerosene lamps flickering in homes along the bayou.

When we reached the creek I could see there were dozens of cars along Oyster Road. Other rowboats were drifting up ahead.

I watched as Raymie and Hank backwatered their oars. I could almost hear the silence. Then I was conscious of the "pullip-pullip" of water lapping against the marsh.

There was no moon, and everything was black and still. I felt hot and sticky in my shorts and halter. It was as if a hand were being held against my mouth and nose.

My eyes strained against the black; the car lights had been turned off, and it was impossible to see.

Raymie's whisper was as startling as a shout.

"There! Over there! See it?"

We did. I realized it was only a short distance above us — a soft blue ball of flame floating several feet above the marsh. It glided near a clump of scrub pine trees, floating eerily. Behind its pale glow of light I could see the face of a man — a man I had seen before!

I screamed! I couldn't help it!

"Let's go back, Raymie!"

"Sit down!" Raymie whispered hoarsely.

I did. I sat on the floor of the skiff. I was miserable. I wondered if Raymie and Hank had seen the face in the marsh. Why had I ever wanted to come? I began to pray that the headless fisherman wouldn't turn his light on me!

Raymie and Hank didn't act afraid at all. They were

whispering plans for rowing up a little inlet to get a close look.

As the skiff turned, the ghostly light began to dip and weave its way to us. It's movement was slow and sure. It trembled and quavered. I held my breath. I felt a tingling all over my body, and my chest hurt from the booming of my heart. There was a soft, strange noise. I was surprised when I realized it was the sound of my own teeth, clicking together.

The flame lingered lightly over the bow, where it stopped for a moment. Then it passed without a sound over the unmoving heads of Raymie and Hank. My heart stopped as it drifted toward me! In a moment it hung, silent and threatening, over my head.

I leaped forward then. My screams tore into that hot, black night. The sudden lurch upset the skiff. A scramble of legs and arms flailed into the air and splashed into the water.

I went down, down, down into a forever of blackness. I knew that I would never come up again. When I did, the skiff was over my head. I would drown! Raymie would be sorry now!

Almost as suddenly, the boat was uprighted. Raymie was lifting me back into the boat, and Hank was grappling for the oars.

It was too much to take. I began to bawl.

Raymie said a four-letter word, and I decided right

then that I'd tell Papa when I got home.

Hank was nicer than usual. He put his arm around me and told me that everything was going to be all right. It was the first time I had ever really liked Hank.

When we were quiet enough to realize it, we saw that the Will-o'-the-Wisp was gone. We heard later that some people waited all night to see it, but it never returned.

At home, Papa told us that the Will-o'-the-Wisp is a mixture of gases from the marsh that causes a flame to float above the ground. Raymie and Hank said they knew it was an evil spirit. I think they knew Papa was right, but it was more thrilling for them to believe their own story.

I was willing to believe Papa about the gases. After all, he was my father, and he never lied to me. But there was something else that I had seen that I couldn't explain. I knew that the face behind that mysterious glow of light belonged to Old Jake. Was I imagining that his arm was pointing frantically back to the mouth of the bayou?

When I finally understood that I should be angry at *myself* for capsizing the boat, instead of Raymie, I decided to tell him about Old Jake. But that's when I really became angry. He didn't believe me. He said I was imagining things, or just making them up. I wished with all my heart that I had told Jeanne' first. I knew that *she* would believe me.

Chapter Four

Strange Happenings at Belle's Hammock

The next morning after breakfast I ran out into the back yard to climb the pecan tree. That was where I always called for Jeanne'.

The idea for a picnic at Belle's Hammock had plopped itself into my head when I woke up that morning. It would be a good chance to tell Jeanne' about Old Jake.

Grits and ham were my favorite breakfast, but this morning I gulped them down, scarcely enjoying the taste.

Mama asked, "Marcie, what on earth is the matter with you?"

"Nmph," I said, because my mouth was stuffed with biscuit, and I was racing down the back steps. The screened door slammed behind me. As I climbed the tree I was singing.

"I'm nine years old today. I'm nine years old today. Hi, ho, the derio, to Belle's Hammock we will stray."

Many times I had dreamed of going to Belle's Hammock the way Raymie and his friends did.

Papa usually said, "You're too young, Marcie, but when you're nine you may go."

I don't know why he said nine, but I wasn't about to question him.

Well, this day I was nine, and Papa never broke his promises. I was going to Belle's Hammock, and I was going to take my best friend with me. I was also going to get to tell her the exciting story of my adventure with the Will-o'-the-Wisp. *She'd* believe me when I told her Old Jake was there!

Belle's Hammock jutted out from the other side of the bayou in a tangle of oak, pine scrubs, and vines, which is what hammock means . . .a sort of woods. Raymie said the leaves were a richer green there, and grew thickly twined together.

I remember how I tingled with the joy of telling Jeanne' my plans.

I fitted my bare toes into the lowest crook of the tree and hoisted myself out onto the limb which hung over the adjoining blackberry field. With my head thrown back, I yodeled my best Tarzan yell. I clutched the branches tightly as I strained to listen. Across the field came Jeanne's answering yodel. I waited. In a few moments she emerged from the vines, flushed and curious in her yellow shorts and halter.

"What's up?"

I told her, stumbling all over my words the way I

always did when my mind and feelings ran ahead of my tongue, but Jeanne' understood me.

"I'll go fix a jug of lemonade, some bread and butter, and whatever else Ma will let me have. I'll be right back."

Mama said we could take leftover fried chicken and some devil's food cake. I threw in a few biscuits, although I didn't really like them cold. The night before Papa had cut some joints of sugar cane for us. As I put them in my sack I thought how beautiful the waxy, purple stalks were.

"Marcie," Mama begged, "please be careful. You could drown or be bitten by a water moccasin."

"Awww, Mama. Nothin's goin' to happen," I said.

We raced across the shell road to the place where Papa's skiff was docked. We loaded our lunches and lemonade. It was hard fitting those long oars into the oarlocks, but today we were strong and capable. I touched bottom with my oar and pushed off with a satisfied grunt.

Papa called to us from the wharf where he was "oiling up" a boat. "Be sure to get back before dark, Marcie."

I lifted one hand from the oar and waved happily. This was going to be a day I'd never forget, I was sure.

"We did it, Jeanne'," I exclaimed as we passed the shop. "They let us go! There's no one to tell us what to do all day, and we'll find out if that old graveyard is as spooky as Raymie says it is."

"What was the secret you were going to tell me?" Jeanne' asked.

That was one reason I liked her so much. She loved a secret as much as I did. I told her the happenings of the night before. I even added a few. I knew she wouldn't mind. She liked a good story. She listened seriously and agreed with me that I *had* seen Old Jake. Hank and Raymie were stupid not to believe me.

Belle's Hammock was across the bayou and around a slight curve. It didn't take us long to get there. I back-watered the oars while Jeanne' tied the rope around an overhanging limb from the oak at the edge of the water.

"C'mon," I yelled as I threw our lunches to a grassy mound on the other side of the tree. "Let's play like we're Tarzan and Jane, and go swining on the grapevines."

Jeanne' yelled, "Okay, but I'm Jane," as she rushed to the tangled mass of trees and brush.

I slid to a stop. "No fair! You got to be Jane last time we played. I wanna be Jane."

"Well, all right!" she steamed. "I'd rather be Tarzan, anyhow. He was friends to all the apes and lions. Who wants to be sissy old Jane? Yah!"

That "yah" made me furious, but I knew we'd spoil our day if I let myself get angry. I took a deep breath and followed.

When we tired of playing Tarzan we built sand castles for the fiddler crabs and pretended they were kings and queens. We climbed trees and picked wild flowers. Finally, we ate our lunch in an old tree fort which had been built in the branches of the tree where our skiff was tied. The thick Spanish moss made our fort a secret.

We talked of finding Old Jake's treasure.

"Jeanne', if we find it, we'll be rich. Since you're my best friend I'll give you at least a hundred, maybe a thousand dollars and then your mama won't have to work at the café anymore. And my mama and papa won't have to work as hard either. Maybe I can send my mama to New York to see a play on the legitimate stage, like Mama is always talking about."

With a wide sweep of my hands I said, "It will be *glorious*!"

I liked the way it came off my tongue, like a storm wave in the gulf.

We kept putting off our visit to the cemetery. In midafternoon I said, "Do you think we ought to get over to the graveyard before it gets too dark?"

"Yeah, we might as well," Jeanne' answered.

I was ashamed because my voice came out kind of small and timid when I said, "Raymie says the trees grow in a real thick circle around the graves. He says it's kind of dark in there, even in the daytime, but I ain't scared, though."

"Me neither," Jeanne' said, and her voice sounded like mine.

We found the cemetery, after a short search.

It was surrounded by trees, just as Raymie had said.

Most of the ten or fifteen graves were overgrown with sumac and wild grape vines. We could barely read the writings on the tombstones. All the names were French, and the dates were very old.

"Look, Marcie!" Jeanne' exclaimed. She pointed to a tombstone that read, "Pierre des Jardins, 1788-1832. Priez pour lui."

I proudly pronounced, "Pee-air day Jar-*dan*. Pree-ay pore lwee. That means, 'Pray for him' in French. Mama taught me."

"Ahhh, look, Marcie. Here's a little baby's grave. It says, 'L'enfant Marie Luise Beauchamp. 1 avril-auguste, 1818. Awww, she was only four months old. Isn't that sad?"

I couldn't help it. My eyes filled with tears. "Her grave says pree-ay pore lwee, too. Do you think we should?"

"'Course," Jeanne' agreed.

We knelt in the grass. I used my most serious prayer voice. "Dear God. Bless all these dear departed ones. And You and the angels, would y'all take care of them, please? Especially Pee-air day Jar-*dan* and Mar*ie* Luise. Ahhh-*men*!"

The air about us was strangely quiet and unmoving. The shadows beyond the trees were dark and oddly shaped.

"Let's go now," Jeanne' suggested, and I said, "Yeah,

we might as well."

We silently picked our way through the weeds and vines to the shore to check on the queens in their castles. Only one crusty old fiddler crab remained. The others had escaped. I picked him up by his back while he wildly waved his pincer.

"Here you are, Your Majesty," I said as I placed him near the water.

We were picking up our empty sacks and lemonade jug when Jeanne' said, "Omigosh! I've lost the locket my daddy gave me for my birthday!"

I had a flash of memory then. "I think I saw it hit my hand when we were praying for Marie Luise. I didn't think of what it was at the time."

"Marcie!" Jeanne' scolded, "You had your eyes open when we prayed!"

I didn't like to admit that, and I was angry to think we would have to return to the cemetery. "It's a good thing I did, I'd say! Okay, let's go back!"

The sun was beginning to go down. Deeper in the hammock it would be darker than before. I tried to sing, but when my voice came out squeaky, I stopped.

"Let's hold hands," Jeanne' suggested.

"Yeah," I agreed, "Let's."

We struggled through the vines and underbrush. The first trip to the cemetery had been easy enough, but now the branches were like gnarled old arms, tearing at our clothes and scratching our bare legs.

We didn't see the man at first. When we reached the cemetery we fell to our knees, concentrating on finding the locket.

I saw the glimmer of silver in the weeds by the baby's grave site.

"Here it is, Jeanne'," I whispered.

"Oh, thank heavans! Why are you whispering?" Jeanne' whispered.

"I don't know," I whispered back. "Why are you whispering?"

When we stood up we saw him.

He was standing near Pierre des Jardin's headstone. His clothes were unfamiliar, but I had seen those eyes before. They were black and wild. He seemed to want to tell us something. He made scooping motions with his hands towards a blackberry bush nearby.

Our screams sliced through the twilight air. Jeanne's fear made her unable to move. I grasped her wrist, using all my strength. I had only one purpose; get out of those woods to our only means of escape, the skiff. We ran!

When we reached the water we stopped in shock. Somehow the knot which had tied our boat to the tree had loosened. The rope dangled from the tree into the water. The skiff was gone.

Had someone deliberately untied it?

"Here, Jeanne'!" I gasped. "Up in the tree!"

We scrambled frantically into the old tree house.

From our perch we could see the hammock on one side and the bayou on the other. We sat back to back, so we could cover both sides.

"Jeanne', it was Old Jake!" I said. "I couldn't tell at first because it was so dark in there. But I'd know those eyes anywhere."

That was the wrong thing to say. Jeanne' began to whimper like a little puppy. I tried to comfort her.

"If he was goin' to come for us, he'd be here already. Besides, maybe he didn't see us."

"Mama and Papa say there's no such thing as ghosts. Besides, Hank and Raymie said Old Jake didn't burn up in the fire."

"Maybe *he* or *it* reached the boat before we did. Maybe he untied our boat. Maybe he'll come back for us."

It isn't easy to comfort someone when you're thinking the same thing they're thinking.

The lights were beginning to flicker on across the bayou. They were of no help to us. They were too far away.

I tried again to make Jeanne' feel better. "The preacher says God takes care of His little children. And Mama and Papa know where we are. They'll come looking for us."

"Maybe," Jeanne' sniveled.

I was quiet then. My eyes searched the bayou for

some shape. By the last light of the sky I could barely make out a shape gliding towards our tree. There was a dark, sinister form of a figure bent over. I could hear the creak of oars and the "puh-lash, puh-lash" of the water above Jeanne's muffled sobs.

Then I recognized him.

"Raymie!" I screamed, which caused him to swerve widely.

"Where in tarnation are you?" he growled angrily. "You stupid nuts don't have the sense you were born with! You have Mama scared to death. She thinks you're drowned! And don't you know how to tie a skiff? Papa said this is the last time in a blue moon you'll ever use his skiff!"

We clambered down the tree and into the skiff.

"Oh, Raymie, you don't know what happened! Oh, *Ray*mie. . ."

In a wild tumble of words we told our story. I didn't appreciate what happened then. Raymie began to laugh. I guess he was sort of hysterical, like maybe he was glad I was alive, but he shouldn't have laughed! He rested the oar handles on his knees, and laughed until the tears ran down his face.

"You little catfish sure do have some imagination!"

I don't know what took hold of me then. I stood up on the skiff and began to hit him with my fists. He held his arms in front of him, still laughing, then he suddenly stopped.

"I'm sorry, Marcie. It's okay, Jeanne'. Hank and I will go over there tomorrow and see what you were talking about. It . . . it just sounded funny."

Papa was really mad at first, but then his eyes twinkled, and he said, "What you probably saw was a grave robber looking for any jewels or valuable ornaments he could find. It's a gruesome thing, but there are some people who do that."

I said, "Maybe it wasn't Old Jake," and Mama looked at me kind of funny, so I said, "I betcha it was the ghost of Pierre des Jardins who came back because of our prayers."

Mama said, "Don't be silly, Marcie, there aren't any ghosts."

The next day Raymie and Hank went over to Belle's Hammock. They said they couldn't find anything unusual, but to be certain, they dug all around Pierre's grave, and especially at the blackberry bush. The treasure wasn't there.

I guess they never would have believed us, but when they went back to their skiff they saw something that convinced them that we had seen Old Jake.

Pinned to the bow of the boat, by an old, rusty fishhook, was the torn remainder of the treasure map!

Chapter Five

Man or Ghost?

About the second week in June, Mr. Jim, the drummer from Strandard Coffee came down from Mobile, as he did every month. I remembered Mr. Jim, because when Mama bought the can of coffee she always let me open it. The reason this was such a treat was because of the big candy cane that was hidden in the coffee. It surprised me every time how good coffee-flavored peppermint stick tasted, and how awful coffee tasted in a cup. I liked café au lait, though, That means coffee with milk. Mama added a teaspoon of sugar, and that was delicious.

I also remember that a few days later Mama had her 4-H Club Meeting at our house. Some 4-H Club members had hogs and cows, but Mama's group mostly did sewing.

Jeanne' and I made up a song about Mrs. O'Reilly. She was the 4-H Club leader who came down from Mobile to lead the meetings She had a wig of red horsehair and she wore a lot of rouge on her cheeks. Mama said she was a very good lady — that she had had typhoid as a little girl and had lost all of her hair. Jeanne' and I thought she was funny because she made round o's with her mouth when she talked and had a habit of using the word consequently.

To the tune of "Little Orphan Annie" we sang:
"Our mothers had a Four-H Club the other day,
And Mrs. O'Reilly came our way
And this is what she said,
About the way we sew our thread.
'Consequently I think so
But consequently I don't know.
Consequently I think so,
But consequently, I don't know.' "

We fell across the bed and rolled to the floor with our laughing.

Mama was upset with us. She came back to my bedroom with her black eyes smoldering. She said that all the ladies could hear us singing. We didn't realize they could hear.

I was sorry. I suppose I was thoughtless because a lot of exciting things had happened at once and now, nothing much was happening at all. I just wanted a little fun.

Raymie got a chance to go on a shrimp boat for two weeks with a friend of Papa's. Then, Jeanne and I got in a big fight and wouldn't speak to each other. I got mad when she said my mama was putting on airs because she was president of the P.T.A. for the coming year and a member of the Women's Missionary Society of the Baptist

Church.

Jeanne's mother had to work as a waitress in a restaurant because her daddy didn't always have a job. I really liked Jeanne's mother, and I know Jeanne' liked Mama, but before you knew it, we were fighting mad. When she pulled my hair, that was the last straw! I decided I would never speak to her again, as long as she lived. Blood sisters or not!

For a while I kept thinking of the pirate's map, and wishing I could figure it out. I wished Raymie would come back right away so we could start searching. It would be fun, being rich. I figured out how we would buy a new car with extra-wide running boards so a lot of friends could hang on when we went simming around on the coast. Maybe I'd buy Mama a red horsehair wig, even if they were funny-looking. I'd also buy her a gold satin and velvet dress, and when Jeanne' saw her in it, she would be sorry she had said anything about such an elegant lady.

A few days later it rained as I had never seen it rain before, and the wind blew so hard that storm warnings were put up. We though we were going to have a hurricane. The sky was yellow-green.

We drove around the coast to see how high the tide had risen. The water was over the coast road, and we had to go slow. Papa was worried about Raymie, but we got a call from Pascagoula, Mississippi, when we came back home that said Mr. Pete and Raymie had docked there, and they were safe. Finally the rains stopped, the winds died, and the storm warnings came down.

While it was raining so hard, the lightning would arc across the sky, showing the twisting trees and wind-bent rain in a glorious flashing instant. Then the thunder would "ba-room," and I could feel the sound in my teeth and through all my bones. Papa took me out on the screened porch and told me there wasn't anything to be afraid of.

He said, "The heavens declare the glory of God, and the firmament showeth His handiwork." When Papa quoted something from the Bible I knew he believed it. Since then, I never have been afraid of storms.

When the stom was over, he took me by the hand and walked down to the hardware store with me. He said he had something he wanted me to see. We walked out onto the wharf, and he pointed to a giant cobweb that had been woven between the two gas pumps. The rain hadn't washed it away. Instead, the oil and water on the silky thread glistened with all the colors of the rainbow.

Those were some of the reasons June passed quickly that summer.

Mama took me to the library two or three times a week. It was a little library, but it had enough books for me. I read a beautiful novel called *Ramona* and made up my mind I would marry a handsome Indian as soon as I was old enough.

Mrs. Pierson, the librarian, told Mama she thought I

was too young to read a love story, but Mama said if I was smart enough to read it, it was all right.

After a few weeks of not seeing Jeanne' I couldn't stand it any longer. I sent her a note by Mr. Aaron, who delivered ice for Mr. Tolly.

It said, "Why don't you come up and see me sometime?" because Mae West had said that in a movie we had seen before our fight.

She came over as soon as she read the note. We felt shy at first, because we remembered swearing we'd never speak to each other for the rest of our lives. But after a while, things were the same as ever.

It was good being friends again, and I asked Mama if Jeanne' could spend the night. Mama said that'd be fine, and we rushed down to Harley's Shrimp and Oyster Café to ask Jeanne's mother. As soon as she said "yes" we went to her house to get her toothbrush and nightgown.

On the way back Jeanne' said, "Mr. Joseph Deauville told my papa he thought he saw Old Jake over by the 'bandoned icehouse the other night. Papa said that couldn't be possible, because Old Jake is dead..."

"Jeanne' Delacorte, if you told our secret I'll never speak to you again," I interrupted.

"I didn't! I promise!" Jeanne' quickly denied. "Anyhow, Mr. Joseph swore it was a dead ringer for Old Jake, and Pa said, "Well, it was his ghost then, because he's deader than a doornail."

"Do you think Old Jake might be stayin' at the 'bandoned ice plant?"

'Well, I've been thinkin' about it, and he could. They don't make ice there anymore, and there isn't anyone around who'd care."

"Yeah, but the new ice plant is next door, and Mr. Tolly would know if there was anything funny going on."

That night we had our chance to go by the old ice-house. Mama asked us to take a recipe to Cousin Cassie who lived on the other side of the road from the new ice plant. We'd just finished a big supper of fried chicken and gravy, and Papa said he had picked up a melon from the icehouse, nice and cold.

"I wish you'd told me, Isaac," Mama said. "I have a recipe for deviled crab that Cuddin Cassie's been asking for, and you could have dropped it off."

Cuddin Cassie was actually cousin Cassie, but we all called her Cuddin Cassie.

"Would you girls mind going up the road to her house? I'll give her a ring on the phone so she'll know you're coming. She'll turn her porch lights on, and you can take Papa's flashlight. Would y'all be scared to do that?"

"Oh, no!" Jeanne' said, and I was just as eager.

"Could we have the watermelon when we get back?" I said. "'Course, honey," Mama said, and she started looking through her papers for the recipe. She finally found it in her King James Bible.

Jeanne' and I skipped down the road. Papa and Mama didn't worry about us; nothing much bad seemed to happen in our town.

But Jeanne' and I were worried in a goose-pimply way. We would have to pass the abandoned icehouse coming and going.

"What does 'bandoned mean?" Jeanne' asked as we carefully followed the light I held before us.

"It means haunted," I said quickly, because I wasn't sure.

We walked hurriedly past the icehouse and ran the remaining several yards to Cuddin Cassie's.

Cousin Cassie met us at the door. She was tall and skinny, and her black hair was pulled tightly back into a small bun at the back of her neck.

"Ain't you girls scared to be out on a dark night like this?"

We had the feeling she wanted us to be afraid.

"No, Ma'am," we both said.

"Well, I have a piece of raisin cake and a glass of milk for you," she said.

We were tempted to have some, but we remembered the piece of watermelon waiting for us at home. We thanked her and waved goodnight as she watched us awhile from the door. Then we saw her light go off and her skinny frame slip back into her house.

The night suddenly became blacker and quieter. We could hear the sounds of bullfrogs and crickets, and nothing else. There were no cars on the shell road tonight; there were no boats moving on the bayou. The newer, more modern icehouse stayed open all night for the boats going out; Mr. Tolly Breame was probably inside. The old, tin house was further back from the road. It was built over the bayou.

We thought we could see the figure of a man standing under the eaves in the far corner, but we couldn't be sure. The darkness and stillness were more than we could stand.

I began to sing: "Be not dismay-ed what-e'er betide, God will take care of you-ou. Beneath his wi-ings of love abide. God will take care of you. He will take care of you. Through all the way. O'er all the day. He will take ca-air of youuuu. God will take ca-air of youuuu."

My high voice squeaked comfortingly in the still night air.

Jeanne' didn't know that song from her Catholic Church, but while I sang I could hear her saying a few "Hail Mary's" under her breath.

Between the two of us, we made it home in time to have watermelon with my folks.

We planned to get Raymie and Hank to go with us to explore the old icehouse as soon as Raymie returned.

Chapter Six

We Begin Our Search

In the middle of one hot July night I heard someone at the door. I had only gotten to sleep after Mama put a fan in my roon. She placed it next to my bed, and the quiet whirring and coolness finally put me to sleep.

It seemed I was only asleep for a short time when I heard Mama say to Papa, "Isaac, what on earth were you thinking of?"

Papa said, "Now, pet, it will only be for a few days, then they'll go. I'll find them a place over in the factory camps as soon as I can get the poor guy a job. Honey, they don't have any place to go."

"Don't call me pet and honey," she said, her black eyes flashing, I knew, even though I couldn't see her.

"Where on earth are we going to put them?"

"Shhh. They'll hear you!" Papa said.

"Well, I don't care if they do," Mama said, but I noticed she whispered this time.

I stumbled to the door, holding my dimity nightgown around me. Mama said I should be modest.

A little balding man stood at the door with his family. He almost didn't have a chin, and his pale blue eyes were watery and sad. I thought that he was crying, but I later realized that his eyes were like that all the time.

His wife was a head taller than he, and twice as big. Their two tangled haired children stared at me, so I stared back.

The woman said, in an oily voice which I didn't like at all, "Oh, Miz He'le'ne, you're the kindest lady I ever knowed. I heard how you helped them little Wannamaker kids, always givin' food 'cause their no-good daddy is f'rever drunk. We ain't goin' to be no trouble, nohow. We'll just lay down on a pallet somewhere in a corner, and we won't eat much at all."

Mama was still furious with Papa, but she said, as politely as she could, "Of course, come in."

The woman, her name was Mrs. Potter, stood there while Mama made a pallet for the children in the living room. She didn't make a move to help, and I could see Mama was trying hard to be calm.

Mama was always kind to children. That's why I was surprised when she pushed the little girl away from her and screamed, "They've got lice! Marcie, go run water in the bathtub! Isaac! Get me a jug of kerosene!"

Mrs. Potter was mumbling something about how she didn't see how any child of *hers* could have gotten lice, and I was taken with a powerful case of itching.

54

The water ran into the tub at what seemed like a slow trickle to me, and I began to side with Mama in my thoughts against Papa. He had no right to cause this misery to descend on us, like some plague from the Bible.

Mama came in the bathroom to check on the water, and I started to tell her what I thought.

She surprised me. She said, "Marcie, you're always saying you want to be a missionary in 'deepest, darkest Africa.' Well, here's your chance to practice."

Mama wiped the perspiration from her forehead with the back of her hand and sighed. "Believe me, Marcie, a person doesn't have to go to Africa or any place *else* to be a missionary! There's plenty to be done right in your home town!"

I didn't agree with her about that, but I did feel ashamed. I went back into the living room and put my arms around the dirty little boy.

"Come on, Honey," I said. I thought I was going to be sick. "Let's get rid of them filthy old lice."

"Those," Mama said.

"What?" I asked.

"Those, not them" she corrected.

Mama corrected my grammar at the craziest times.

Between the two of us, the kerosene, some water, a bar of Octagon soap and a fine-toothed comb, we got that whole family rid of lice before Mama would let anyone sleep in her house. The most horrible part of it all was that when they left, three days later, Mama found one of those filthy creatures crawling on me. I wanted to die. I sobbed while she put me through the same treatment the Potters had gone through.

Raymie came home after Mama had to de-lice me. I made her promise not to tell him.

I never was so glad to see anyone. I didn't know how I could want so badly to see anyone who spent all his waking hours teasing me. I was anxious to tell him about Joseph Deauville thinking he'd seen Old Jake at the abandoned icehouse.

Raymie had a lot to tell first. The fishing boat he had been on had almost capsized in the storm. Later, there was a fire in the engine, but they put it out. And they brought in a big haul of shrimp. Mr. Pete paid him extra money because he was such a good help, but Papa said he couldn't go again this year; he was needed too badly in the shop.

As soon as we had a chance to be alone, I told him about Mr. Joseph.

"No kidding?" he said. "You know, Marcie, I've been thinking about the map while I've been away. I think I've figured out where the treasure is. That corner piece Mr. Jake didn't give us until later, well, that shows the mouth of the bayou at Indian Hill — maybe under the old oak tree that's on top, or near the artesian well that's at the bottom. The reason we've been confused is that there's been a lot of building since then — all the factories, camps, docks and houses. Other things have changed, too. The tree and the hill probably had French or Indian names. But the way the bayou curves — that's the way it does on the map. That's the way it does on the map, sure as shootin'."

"When can we go explore?" I asked.

"Marcie, you're too little to help with that."

"Oh, no, you don't!" I cried. I could feel my blood hot and boiling under my skin.

Raymie lifted his palms and his shoulders and said, "All right. All *right*!"

My hands were on my hips. I lifted my chin up and then down in a satisfied motion.

"I should think so!" I said, really using my lips. "I'm going to tell Jeanne' right away."

I called her from the phone on the back porch.

"Tell her we'll meet her next Sunday before we go to B.T.U." That stood for Baptist Training Union. It was a kind of Sunday School at night.

Papa usually opened the shop on Sunday afternoons during the shrimp and oyster season, but he didn't like us to go to the picture show on the Sabbath. He said if Raymie had some place he wanted us to go, we could leave at five o'clock, as long as we were back for B.T.U. at seven.

Hank and Jeanne' met us at the shop as soon as Papa closed. Both Hank and Raymie had shovels, and Raymie carried a big gunny sack. The sight of that gunny sack thrilled me; it meant the possibility of treasure discovered.

This time we rowed in the oposite direction from the creek, Big Bridge, and Old Jake's house. As we rowed behind the abandoned icehouse, I suddenly had a flash of memory. I remembered Old Jake in the marsh, waving frantically in this direction. Maybe that's what he had meant.

Raymie said, "Jeanne', do you think old man Deauville really saw Old Jake?"

"He sounded plum serious, Raymie," Jeanne' said, "He was over to the house again on Saturday, and he was still talking about it."

Hank said, "After we look for the treasure awhile, maybe we could stop by the icehouse and see."

"We won't have any time tonight," Raymie said, "but maybe we can come back next week."

"Do you think old Jake is crazy?" Jeanne' asked.

"He may have *been* crazy, but I think he's a ghost now," Hank answered.

"Aww, Hank, there aren't any such things as ghosts," Raymie said, but he didn't sound very sure.

For some reason we didn't talk much after that. The boys rowed smoothly. When their oars dipped into the water, it made me think of how it is when you put a spoon into a jar of molasses.

Bayou water always seems blacker than other streams, maybe because it has little current, and it is brackish. Everytime we rowed into the mouth of the bayou I felt a special thrill. The bayou seemed secure; my father's store and our house were both on the bayou. Also, it was a fairly narrow stream. Even at the widest part you could yell across to someone on the other shore.

The bay was different. Once you were out far enough, you couldn't see the shore. The bay was almost always a golden beige color. It wasn't until you got out into the gulf that you saw blue and turquoise colors like you see in pictures. At the place where the bayou widened into the bay the water became a steel gray, and little ripples were seen on the surface.

That's how it was at the mouth as we left the factories and wharves. There were waves of dark green marsh on either side of us. As we rounded the curve that would take us out into the bay we could see Indian Hill on our right.

It wasn't really a hill. It was a mound of dirt covered with grass. We had been told these old mounds were Indian burial grounds, and all of us kids had found arrowheads there.

Jeanne' and I gasped with pleasure when we saw hundreds of little coffee bean trees dripping with orange grape-like clusters of blossoms. I don't think the boys noticed. We would have loved to pick armfuls, but we knew the boys would be disgusted with us. We didn't want to take any chance of doing anything that would make them sorry they had taken us along. I scribbled a note on my brain to come back someday with Jeanne'. It would be a perfect place to pretend we were fairyland princesses.

Papa said Raymie was a born leader, and if being bossy was any proof, he sure was right. Once we were on land he had us all roping off sections of ground, measuring distances, and running errands back and forth between the boat and the tree. We didn't really mind this time; we were too excited.

We couldn't believe how fast the time went. Raymie had borrowed Papa's watch. It made him feel important to pull it out of his pocket and check the time.

We weren't having any luck, though. Raymie and Hank had that mound criss-crossed with ditches, and we couldn't find anything but arrowheads.

There was an artesian well at the foot of the mound. Papa told me artesian wells weren't like other wells such as people dug in the ground. Water just spurts out of the surface of the ground on its own pressure. The one at Indian Hill shot into the air about three feet. The water reminded me of the cut-glass vase Grandma Delaune had given Mama. The sunlight made it shine like crystal rock. It looked like it would be delicious, but I didn't like the taste. Its gushing sounded like a roaring river, but a little more muffled. We had to speak loudly to be heard above it.

I guess I was the first one to hear the voice. I looked around to figure out where it was coming from. That's when I saw that Cajun woman who had moved to Bayou La Batre a few years before. Her home had been in Houma, Louisiana.She came over with her husband who was a part of a crew of men who dredged the bayou. Every so often the bayou would need to be dug out to make it deeper for the larger fishing boats. Her husband had been killed in an accident on the dredging barge.

After his death she lived near the mound in a little shack across the marsh. There was a little garden and some hogs, and she did a lot of crabbing and fishing. Mama worried about how she kept herself alive.

Everyday she came into Bayou La Batre with two big buckets balanced on either side, and collected slops for her hogs. She had a smile for everyone.

It wasn't easy to understand her when she spoke. Her Cajun accent was thicker than Old Jake's. She was called "Slop Betsy." I suppose it wasn't respectful, but even she expected all of us to call her that.

The others didn't hear her at first, so I finally went over and pulled at Raymie's sleeve.

"Raymie, it's "Slop Betsy." She's trying to tell us something."

Raymie wiped the sweat from his face with one arm, and stared at "Slop Betsy." She grinned at him, and shoved a mass of oily, black curls from her eyes.

"Allo! Old Jake, he say 'C'est près d'eau,' you unnerstan'? He say, you dig, then he come."

"What . . . what do you mean?" Raymie asked, puzzled.

I was the one who figured it out. Those French words Mama was always trying to teach us came in handy.

"Près d'eau! She means near the water! She means the well!"

I turned to her. "But, who . . . how . . . what do you know about Old Jake? Where is he? Is he alive?"

"Slop Betsy" smiled, and a million wrinkles creased her sun-browned cheeks, "Old Jake, he tell you dig!" She turned and walked away.

"Please. Come back. Do you know Old Jake? Is he crazy? If we find the treasure will he put some kind of spell on us? Won't you answer us?" I cried.

"Slop Betsy" tossed her thick, matted hair, lifted her palms to the sky, and said, "Me, I no unnerstan'."

But then, as she walked away, she began to laugh, a wild laugh that left the four of us frightened and puzzled.

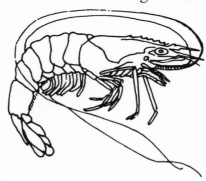

Chapter Seven

De Tra-sure, It is Find

We stood staring after "Slop Betsy" with unbelieving eyes.

Hank finally said, "What time is it?"

Raymie fumbled for his watch.

"Yeah, we'd better go. We're already late for B.T.U."

"Hurry, then!" I said. I hated to disobey Mama and Papa, because they always trusted us.

We dragged the shovels, rulers, and other things back into the skiff. Jeanne' and I settled ourselves on the seat in the stern. We were disappointed and unhappy.

"We'll try after supper tomorrow night," Raymie said.

"We won't be able to see a thing," Hank said.

"I can bring two flashlights," Jeanne' offered.

"We can borrow that big lantern from Papa, Raymie," I said.

"Papa's going to wonder what we're doing with all these lights and shovels. Maybe we ought to tell him," Raymie said.

We all agreed that maybe we would tell him about searching for treasure, but not about Old Jake yet.

"Isn't that d'ceivin' him?" I asked.

"I don't think so," Raymie answered. "I think he'll understand, especially when we come home rich."

"Do you think 'Slop Betsy' knows Old Jake?" Jeanne' wanted to know.

"There ain't no doubt about it!" Hank answered.

"*Isn't any,*" I corrected, but Hank gave me a disgusted look, and ignored me.

Raymie said, "She was even telling us where to dig. Tomorrow we'll dig all around that old well. He knows something. Only thing, I can't figure why he wants us to do all the work for him."

I remembered Old Jake's stooped back and slow movements.

"I don't think he's strong enough to do it," I said.

"You're right! Marcie, every once in a while you come up with something that makes me think you have a little sense in that nine-year-old brain, after all!" Hank exclaimed.

"Hmph!" I said. I wondered why I ever thought I had liked him that night at the Will-o'-the-Wisp. And to think I ever considered marrying him someday, instead of a handsome Indian, like Ramona did in the book.

"You're not so smart yourself, Hank Thompson!" I said, and I made the ugliest face I could.

"Oh, shut up, Marcie!" Raymie said.

Jeanne' put her arm around me.

"Don't you say 'shut up' to my best friend!"

Raymie raised an oar and held it above us for an instant. I knew he would never hit us, but I shut up anyway.

Finally, I said, in a small voice, "Mrs. Land says I am one of the brightest children in the class."

"I never heard her say that!" Jeanne' said.

Now I had all three of them against me, and things were even worse when we got home. We were thirty minutes late for B.T.U., there was a note from Mama and Papa that said, "Don't leave this house to go anywhere," and when they got home they told us we wouldn't be going anywhere for a whole *week!*

We didn't argue. We had said we'd be back on time, and we had broken our promise.

That was the longest week I ever spent in my life.

Raymie told Papa we had found a treasure map, and we would like to go back to Indian Hill as soon as our week of punishment was up. Papa didn't ask any questions. In fact, he sort of smiled the way grown-ups do when they think their children are doing something they think is foolish or useless. I was anxious to prove he was wrong about us. It made the week go even slower, being so anxious to prove him wrong.

The day finally came, though. I think I must have

gone down to the shop a hundred times that day to talk to Raymie. Papa told me to please go up to the house and help Mama bake a cake, shell some peas, shuck some corn, or anything! I understood. I knew when I wasn't wanted.

Mama did have some lima beans for me to shell. She cooked a big pot of them for supper, and she made some corn bread. We had my favorite: cold boiled shrimp in their shells. We shelled our own. I had a bigger pile of shells on my plate than anyone.

Then Papa said, "I wish you kids would hurry and get out of here. I've never seen you so fidgety." I think they were glad we were going out. Raymie always played the radio too loud.

I was even more excited than I was when we went to the Will-o'-the-Wisp. I kept holding onto my neck, because I was afraid my heart was going to jump out at that spot. I thought I had a special problem until I told Jeanne' about it, and she said her heart did that when she got excited, too.

We borrowed the big lantern from Papa, and all of us carried a big supply of flashlights, spades, and hoes, I cut four pieces of pound cake for energy and brought a blanket for Jeanne' and me to rest on.

We couldn't stop giggling. For some reason the boys didn't mind this time. They were silly, too. Raymie brought up that old joke about Hank "*hank*-ering" for the girl from

Biloxi again.

Hank said he had fifteen cents, so we stopped at the ice plant wharf to buy a watermelon. Mr. Tolly was "icing up" a shrimp boat. He said we could wait on ourselves. We all loved going into that cold storage room. The watermelons and cold drinks were kept in a little side room where the temperature wasn't as cold. Raymie said they'd freeze and be no good to eat if they were kept where the ice blocks were kept. I'd been in the ice plant with Papa. I liked the smell of the wet sawdust, and the great blocks of crystal ice were beautiful to see.

The warm air felt good on our bare arms after the freezing cold of the ice plant. I was happy and glad to be alive, and I knew my brother and our friends felt that way, too.

We sang "Old Rugged Cross" and "A Spanish Cavalier Stood on His Retreat," and we almost capsized from laughing when Raymie said, "Stood on his *what?*"

Then we sang "Going to Alabama with a Banjo on My Knee." By the time we arrived at the mouth of the bayou our throats were sore and our stomachs were hungry. We docked the boat and ran over to the gushing well to drink, although none of us liked the taste of the artesian water. I surprised everyone with pieces of pound cake. We sat down and enjoyed the rich, buttery goodness. We decided to save the watermelon for later.

Raymie stretched like Papa does after a full meal,

went over to the boat, and began taking out our lanterns and shovels. We could see he meant to get to work and went over to do our share of carrying things from the boat. Raymie and Hank set up the lanterns. Then Raymie sat me on a tree stump with one flashlight, and hoisted Jeanne' onto a low overhanging branch with another.

"Keep the lights trained right where we tell you to. Okay, girls?"

"Don't you need us to dig any?" Jeanne' asked.

Raymie kindly said, "Well, we need you to, but we need the light more."

They began to dig. They started out from the tree stump, where I was sitting, and went in a slow, deep circle around the tree. July nights in Alabama don't cool off, and soon their faces and clothes were wet with perspiration. I felt sorry for them. They dug for about an hour, and they were beginning to breathe hard. I knew they were both strong. They played football and basketball at school, not to mention how hard they both worked — Raymie for Papa, and Hank over at Beaudreaux's shrimp factory.

"Let's have a piece of watermelon," I suggested, and Jeanne' was down from that tree faster than the boys could stop digging.

"Good idea!" she said, and headed for the boat to get the melon and the knife.

Raymie was right behind her. "That melon's too heavy, Jeanne', and you could slip with the knife."

The boys put the melon on the blanket, and we went to work on it. By the time we had finished, Hank and Raymie were sticky with melon seeds and juice. I hardly ever remember a time when we ate a melon outside that we didn't end it with someone having a watermelon fight.

This one didn't last long. We were all too interested in finding the treasure.

A few minutes later Raymie was pushing his foot hard on that shovel again. He was irritated.

"Looks like we've hit a root."

I held the light down into the hole he had made.

"Raymie!" I screamed. "That isn't a root! That's a trunk! A chest! Look! It has metal around the corners."

We all went on our hands and knees around the hole. Hank held onto Raymie to keep from falling in the rushing water. I dropped my flashlight, and when Jeanne' tried to beam her light on the trunk, she bumped into me and dropped hers, too.

"Oh, for Pete's sake!" Raymie roared. "Marcie! Jeanne'! Move back! Here, Hank! You hold the lantern. Just forget the flashlights for a minute. Lemme dig all around it."

He picked up the shovel again. Over and over he repeated the digging movement, foot on shovel, dip, dirt pushed aside. Jeanne' and I stood, scarcely breathing, watching him. We could gradually see the form of a chest taking shape.

Then Raymie said, "Marcie! Jeanne'! Hold the light for Hank so he can help me lift this! Hank, get on the other side!"

There was no doubt about what we had found. It was an old trunk, dirt-caked, of course, but there was no mistaking the shape of it. We leaned forward to see if we could help Raymie lift the lid — it was no use. The lock wouldn't budge.

"Even if we had the key it wouldn't open," Raymie said. "It's sealed by dirt and rust. Besides, we don't want to ruin it. The trunk might be valuable itself."

"Another thing," Hank said, "It may have some breakable objects, like those old crystal chandeliers."

"Yeahhh. . ." Jeanne' and I breathed at the same time. Even at a time like this we had to follow our old routine.

We crooked our right hand little fingers together.

"Pins," I said.

"Needles," she said.

"What goes up the chimney?"

"Smoke."

"Oh, good Lord!" Raymie moaned prayerfully.

"Well," I explained, looking down my nose at him, "something bad could happen to us if we don't do that when we say the same word at the same time."

"And we especially don't want anything bad to happen now," Jeanne' said.

"Maybe they're right," Hank offered.

Raymie said, "Do you think there might be another trunk buried around here some place?"

Hank said he didn't think so, and Raymie agreed they had dug up almost every square foot of the hill.

"Let's get this thing on the boat," Raymie said.

It took all four of us to hoist that trunk into the skiff. It was heavy. Then the boys picked up all the shovels and other tools we had used. Jeanne' and I gathered the flashlights and the blanket.

We became quiet then. I began to have an eerie feeling of being watched. The boys put the big lantern out because it made too much glare for them to row by. Jeanne' and I held onto our flashlights, and occasionally we'd search the surrounding marsh with their beams.

Finally satisfied we were alone, we sat in our seats, still excited, but suddenly very tired. Raymie pushed off from shore with a mighty heave; the trunk made our skiff sit low in the water.

"You girls sit still. Our load is too heavy for the skiff, and it wouldn't take much for us to tip over," he warned.

I remembered that night at the head of the bayou and promised we wouldn't move.

Together the boys dipped their oars, and we slowly moved away from the shore.

When the voice called to us I felt a million pins sticking all over me. It was worse than goose pimples.

It had to be the voice of Old Jake.

"You no forget Ole Jake?" It was a question and a command.

Raymie and Hank backwatered quickly. We came to a stop. We could hear only the muffled roar of the artesian well and our own breathing.

"Old Jake! I mean, Mr. Jake!" Raymie called.

There was no answer.

"Mr. Jake, sir! Won't you please answer us? We need to talk to you."

Silence.

"Let's go, Raymie," Jeanne' whimpered.

"Yeah, Raymie, it's getting late," I whispered.

Raymie and Hank began to row again, and we started back up the bayou toward home.

Chapter Eight

The Voice of Mystery

It was late when we arrived at the dock of the hardware store. We unloaded our tools and other supplies, and Raymie sent me up to the house to get Mama and Papa.

"Tell them we found the treasure we're looking for," he said.

Brother Landry was getting in his car when I crossed the road.

"Ev'ning, Brother Landry," I said. "Is the meetin' over?"

"Ev'ning, Miss Marcie," he answered. "Yes, we've got a swell social planned. Ask Miss He'le'ne about it."

"Yes, sir," I said politely. I didn't think we should let on to anyone about the treasure yet.

I watched his car move away and then rushed into the house.

"Mama! Papa!" I screamed. "We've found the treasure! We've found the treasure!! We went to Old Jake's house one night, and I know we shouldn't have done it, but then he gave us the map on a butcher knife, and we didn't mean any harm, honest . . and then . . ."

Mama and Papa looked at me as if I'd lost all good sense, and then I realized I wasn't making any, so I said weakly, "Come see what we found."

Without saying a word they followed me out of the house, across the road, and to the skiff.

Raymie and Hank pointed to the chest, and Jeanne' said, "Miss He'le'ne, Mr. Isaac; we're all going to be rich."

Of course, then, they had a million questions, and everyone started talking at once.

Raymie and Hank pointed to the chest, and Jeanne' said, "Miss He'le'ne, Mr. Isaac, we're all going to be rich."

Jeanne' and I were quiet then, and we let the boys tell the story.

We drove Jeanne' up the little lane that led to her house, and Hank said he'd cut across the lot to his house.

"It's quicker," he said.

"Are you sure, now? It's no trouble, Hank."

"Yes, sir," Hank said.

Hank slapped Raymie on the shoulder and said, "Looks like we did it, old buddy."

Papa said, "Now you fellows have another job to do."

They looked at him, and he said, "You have to find Old Jake."

"Papa, I think that old man is whacky. If you could

75

see how wild he looks now — and his hair! His eyes are just plain spooky."

Hank agreed. "Yes, sir! That ole guy is goofy, Mr. Dudley. We don't know what he would do if we found him!"

Jeanne' said, "Tell your papa about his fingernails, Marcie."

"I'm sure all those things are true," Papa said, "but actually, you wouldn't have the treasure if it weren't for him."

"Where'll we look?" Raymie asked, and Papa said, "From what you've told me, I'd try the old icehouse first, although I don't think it likely you'll find him there. He may hang around there in the daytime, though."

"Can Raymie get off after work tomorrow?" Hank asked.

"First, we'll have Miss Hélène call the Mobile Historical Society to come down and look at the trunk, and then you can tell Old Jake to come watch them open it."

"Miss" Therese', Jeanne's mama, waved to us to let us know that Jeanne' had gotten in the house all right, and we drove back home.

I didn't sleep all night. The sheets were damp, the way they usually are in the summer, but you don't notice that when you're sleepy. I kept kicking them off.

When I would doze off, I'd awaken with nightmares of Old Jake chasing me around the kitchen table at his house, or I'd see his head floating above the Will-o'-the-Wisp.

Jeanne' came over the next morning, and we listened as Mama called the Mobile Historical Society. They said there was an archeologist from the University of Alabama visiting in Mobile, and he would come down with the president of the society.

That was Tuesday, and the man said they couldn't come till Wednesday afternoon. Mama said we wouldn't touch anything until they came.

Meanwhile, we spent all of our time talking about how we'd look for Old Jake when the boys got off work.

"If they think they're going to look for him without us they're nuts," I told Jeanne'.

"Marcie, maybe we oughta let Hank and Raymie go by themselves," she said.

"Not me! I'm not!" I said. I'd been in on this thing from the beginning, and I wasn't going to back down now. "I think you've got a yellow streak running down your back," I said. I was sorry as soon as I had said it. Not having any sleep had made me cranky.

Jeanne' was furious. "Well, I'm *not* a coward, Miss Priss!" she snapped, and I knew this was going to be another one of our red-hot quarrels.

"You certainly weren't very brave at Belle's Hammock!" I said, trying to be as nasty as possible.

"*You* were te*rrr*ibly brave," she said, acting like she

thought she was a queen or something.

"I was braver than you were. You were howling like somebody's old hound dog!"

"You take that back, Marcie, or I'll never speak to you again!"

"Well, don't, Your Majesty, 'cause I don't prefer to hear the sound of your voice, anyhow!"

She left, her head in the air, her shoulder blades almost touching in the back.

Then Hank called to say he couldn't help, because Mr. Beaudreaux needed him to work that night.

That's how it turned out that finding Old Jake was left to Raymie and me.

Mama said, "Isaac, I don't think these children ought to go looking for that man alone. He sounds dangerous to me. No telling what he might do if he's not right in his mind."

"Raymie's a big boy now, Mama, and it doesn't get dark until late. If they have a problem, they can yell. The icehouse isn't that far away.

"Raymie can go alone, or better still, you can go with him," she suggested.

Papa said, "No, this is a problem they got themselves into, and I think they need to find Old Jake alone."

"I'm going, too, Mama," I said. I was scared, but there wasn't *any way* I'd be left out.

"You'll look out for Marcie, won't you, Raymie?"

Papa asked, and Raymie said, "Sure" in an offhand way that made me realize Raymie was a little bit afraid, too.

When we were ready to leave, Mama stood at the door looking worried and nervous, but Papa looked as though he were trying not to smile. For a moment I wondered if Mama loved us more than Papa did, but then I knew that couldn't be true. I decided it was just that mothers worry more than fathers.

"We'd be glad to have you come along, Papa," I invited.

He said, "Thank you, but I think you and Raymie can handle this just fine."

Walking down to the icehouse with Raymie I felt smaller than I had in a long time. I even began to wonder if I had shrunk some. And another funny thing! I'd been thinking lately that Raymie was a big fellow, but *he* didn't look very big now, either.

"Where do you think we should look first?" I asked.

"How about that little room where they used to have the counter?" Raymie said.

The sun was still shining brightly at six o'clock, but when we opened the creaky wooden door, we realized the old plant was as dark as night inside. There were no windows, and of course, there were no lights in the old building.

I caught hold of Raymie's shirttail and held on tightly. He held the flashlight high above his head and moved its ray slowly around the little room. There was no one there! Something ran across my foot, and I turned to run.

Raymie stopped me. "It's only a mouse, silly." He put his hand on my shoulder. "Here," he said, "let's go into the room where they used to make the ice."

We moved slowly. Some of the boards were broken, and across the room we could see small chunks of light coming through the floor boards.

"Be careful, if any of these boards are out, we could fall through into the water," Raymie warned.

"Mr. Jake!" Raymie called, and in my smaller voice, I echoed, "Mr. Jake!"

There was the sound of lapping water and our breathing.

I called, "Mr. Jake, if you're in here, would you please answer? We've found the treasure, and we want to share it with you."

There was no answer. Then I faintly heard a dry, hacking cough.

"Did you hear that?" I whispered to Raymie.

"What?" he asked.

I guessed he hadn't heard it. Maybe I hadn't heard it, either. Then we both heard it, and there was no mistake. It was the sound a person makes when he's trying not to cough. Funny thing though, it didn't sound like it came from the room we were in.

"Mr. Jake! Is that you?" Raymie asked, and I wished

he sounded braver.

"Please, Mr. Jake, sir," I begged, and my voice didn't sound very brave, either. "Our papa said we wouldn't have found the treasure without you, and we want to share it with you."

He answered then, "You don' come no closer, s'il vous plaît. When you gon' open de tra-sure, hah? You come tell me when you open, then I come."

"There's a man coming to tell us what it's worth tomorrow," Raymie said.

We were straining to see where he was in the darkened room. Our eyes were getting used to the dark, and we could tell that he was nowhere in our sight.

"Mr. Jake, sir," I asked, "are you a ghost?"

He said, "After people leave, you tell Old Jake, then he come."

I could picture his sunken eyes and his curved fingernails.

"Are you a ghost?" I asked again. Of course, he had to be. He was invisible.

The sound of his shrill laughter followed us as we bolted from the room and into the happy relief of open air and sunshine.

Chapter Nine

De Tra-sure, It Is Open

When we got back to the house, Mama was sitting in the swing waiting for us. Papa was lounging on the steps, smoking his cigar, acting like he had forgotten all about us.

We told them all that had happened. That is, all except how we ran when Jake started laughing. That didn't seem important to the story.

Mama said she had a mess of turnip greens waiting on the stove, and oh, yes, she'd baked a sweet potato pie and some corn bread for the pot "likker." The pot liquor was the juice from the greens; it tasted great over corn bread in a bowl.

We drank lots of ice tea, and Mama said, "Why don't we call Jeanne' and Hank over and celebrate with some ice cream?"

Homemade ice cream won out over the argument we'd had the day before, and Jeanne' was at my house in no time.

Raymie got the freezer and ice cream salt out of the tool shed out back, and Papa went down to the shop to get a burlap sack to put over the top for one person to sit on while the other turned the crank.

Mama got cream, eggs, sugar, and vanilla, and started beating, stirring and straining.

Papa said, "Come on, girls, let's go down to the ice plant to get a block of ice."

We piled into the faded blue Dodge, giggling and full of thoughts of our good life: ice cream tonight, riches tomorrow. While Papa went in to get the ice, we looked at the old plant and wondered what Old Jake was doing.

"He has to be a ghost, Jeanne'," I said. "He wasn't anywhere to be seen."

"You told me there's no such things as ghosts, and now you've changed your mind."

"Jeanne'," I explained, "I'm six months older than you are, and a person learns a lot in six months!"

Really good homemade ice cream coats the roof of your mouth with cream and hurts the sides of your head above your eyes when you take a big bite. This was Mama's best. As we ate, we talked of what we might find when we opened the chest.

When it was time for Hank and Jeanne' to leave, Mama said, "Remember, be here at two o'clock. Mr. Rooney said they'd be here at two, and we don't want to delay them."

Papa laughed. "I can tell you this is one time no one will be late. Listen, kids, you don't have to be here at two this morning. Afternoon will be just fine."

Lena, the black woman from Dixon's Corner, came early to help Mama with the wash. Papa had bought a washing machine, but they still put all the clothes through the wringer by hand, and then hung everything on the clothesline strung up between the pecan trees.

At one o'clock Lena suggested that Mama go on into the house.

"You better git in there an' take your bath before them folks git here. You don' want them to think you're poor white trash."

Mama smiled. "I guess you're right, Lena. Thanks. Do you think you can finish by yourself?"

"Yes, ma'am, I sure kin. I ain't even sure I'll be seeing you folks again if you gits all that money Miss Marcie plans on gittin'."

I didn't like the way they laughed.

By one-thirty we were all bathed and ready. Raymie and Papa got someone to stay at the shop while they came up to the house.

While Mama cut a bouquet of zinnias for the dining

room I sat waiting in the swing. I was admiring the crepe myrtle tree in the corner of the yard. It was larger than most crepe myrtles, because it was quite old. Also, there was something unusual about it. It was covered with Spanish moss. Spanish moss usually grew on oaks.

Mama said moss is not really a parasite. It doesn't live off the tree that it grows on. It lives off the air. She said it wouldn't kill the tree. I was glad to hear that. The crinkly pink blossoms were as thick as the moss, and the beauty of the pink and gray tangled together this way filled me with a happiness I couldn't understand.

I was sitting there thinking of how lucky I was to live in this little town. I looked at the giant pink and lavendar hydrangea blossoms by the porch steps — the ragged yellows, reds, and oranges of the zinnias growing on either side of the walk. Then my eyes drifted over to the magnolia at the gate. I lifted my head to follow the line of the shell-white road leading to Papa's shop, the oil darkened wharf, and the black bayou beyond.

Now, in addition to these riches, we would have other things; maybe a new car, more help for Mama in the house, and a full time man to work for Papa in the shop so he would have some time to rest. If Raymie didn't get a football scholarship, maybe he could go to the University of Alabama anyhow. As for me, I imagined a pale blue organdy dress with a matching bow for my hair. Of course, I'd have to let my short hair grow out, maybe even get one of those curling irons to curl it.

I didn't see the shiny Chevrolet coupe which came to a stop underneath the magnolia tree. When I did, I quickly said the good luck jingle that Jeanne' and I always said when we saw a Chevrolet coupe:

"Chevrolet cou-pay

Gumbo fee-lay."

At the same time, I could hear Mama at the back door saying, "Come in, Jeanne', Hank."

"Mama, they're here," I called.

To the lady I said, "Are y'all from the Historical Society?"

"Yes, we are, honey," she said. "Is your mother here?"

I felt very shy. "Yes, ma'am, y'all come on in."

Mama met us at the door.

"Hello, I'm Mrs. Dudley," she said.

The lady said "I'm Mrs. Teague. This is Mr. Rooney, the archeologist, and this gentleman is a locksmith, Mr. Johnson."

Then Mama introduced all of us.

Papa and Raymie went to the back porch to get the chest.

Mr. Johnson said we should put a canvas down so we wouldn't hurt the living room floor. While the rest of us helped spread the canvas out, Mr. Johnson went out to the car to get his tools.

86

Mama asked if anyone would like coffee or lemonade with devil's food cake. That was probably the first time in my life I ever said "no" to chocolate cake, except that time I had the measles.

The grownups talked about how we found the treasure, the weather, and the recipe for devil's food cake, but we four kids just stared at Mr. Johnson.

He worked with all sorts of keys first, but then he said the lock was so rusted it wouldn't do any good to make a key. He took out some sort of chisel and began to work at prying the lid off. It didn't look like it was going to budge.

"It's corroded," he said, whatever that meant.

Papa said he had a tool down at the shop that might help, and we sat quietly waiting while everyone ate cake.

Papa came back with the tool, and Mr. Johnson started again. This time, as he began to move the lid, we all became quiet. We could hear the sounds of metal on metal, and Mr. Johnson took his coat off.

Mama fixed the fan so he'd get the most breeze. I took a cardboard Coca Cola hand fan from the piano and started fanning the other side of him where the electric fan wasn't reaching. As far as I was concerned, Mr. Johnson was more important than the archeologist or the president of the Historical Society. He was the one who would give us the first glimpse of our treasure!

There was a mournful creak, and with a grunt Mr. Johnson lifted the lid!

We all leaned forward, hands to mouth, eyes wide.

I don't know what we expected to see. Hank's remark about candelabra sketched a picture in my mind of crystal and gold, maybe rubies and emeralds, like those in the pirate stories I had read.

The chest was filled with stacks of yellowed paper money!

"Whoopee!" Raymie yelled, and then the rest of us could see what a good thing this could be. There was certainly enough money for the four of us, and Old Jake, too! We joined hands and began to dance around the room.

It took us a few moments to notice that Mama and Papa and our visitors didn't share our excitement. Weren't they happy that we were going to be rich?

I looked at Mama. She looked sad.

"Don't worry, Mama," I said. "I'll share it with the children from deepest, darkest Africa, and I'll never forget my poor, less fortunate friends."

Papa was saying to the archeologist, "Isn't there any value to the money just because of its age?"

"Mr. Dudley, it isn't even that old. It was probably buried sometime around 1865, and this is 1932. That's only 67 years old . . . not really an antique yet. There's a lot of Confederate money floating around. It's worthless. I'm sorry. And the chest is too damaged to be of any value, even as an interesting piece of furniture.

"That's not true!" I said, ready to cry.

Papa put his arm around me, and with his other arm he pulled Jeanne' close to him.

He scolded me, "Marcie, I know you didn't mean to be rude to Mr. Rooney." Then, in a soft voice, he said, "I'm sorry, little ladies, but I'm afraid you're doomed to stay as poor as you already are."

Raymie said, "But it can't be Confederate money! The map is old. It's a map of Jean Lafitte's treasure."

"Did it say that, son? Or did you just hope it? I'm afraid the map is worthless, too. Maybe if you had discussed it with me . . ." Papa said.

"Old Jake thinks it's worth something. I can tell," I said, but then I asked, "You don't think he was trying to trick us all, do you?"

"I don't know, honey," he said. "Maybe we can find out more about it later, but I think we've already taken up too much of these folks' time."

Everyone shook hands, and the visitors told us they were sorry, that this sort of thing happened all the time, and we were not to be embarrassed about it. They couldn't have known how my heart ached.

They left in their Chevrolet, and I didn't bother to say the jingle for good luck. It seemed to me that all our good luck had left us.

While the sun was shining it began to drizzle, not even enough rain to make the sidewalk wet. Usually, that was one of my favorite times. That day, I wouldn't look when they told me a rainbow had arched across the sky, and the "pot of gold" was just on the other side of the bayou.

Jeanne' and I didn't feel like talking, so she went home. Hank left, too, and Papa and Raymie went down to the shop. Mama went into the kitchen to start supper, and I lay on the sofa in the living room under the cool whirring of the fan. Things were throat-aching miserable.

I'd been living on excitement all week. I didn't realize how tired I was. My eyes closed, and I sank into a deep sleep.

When I awakened I was aware that Mama, Papa, and Raymie were having supper. It was around eight, I figured, because the sun had gone down.

I heard Mama say, "Poor little thing . . . Raymie, we'll only be over at the church about an hour and a half. Get her something to eat when she wakes up and, Raymie, try to make her feel better."

It was best to pretend sleep. I didn't want to face their pity. I must have been exhausted, because as soon as I heard the car leave, I slept again. When I awakened I could hear Raymie puttering around in the kitchen.

As I walked into the kitchen I noticed the folks had left the front door open to let in a little breeze.

Standing behind the screened door was the unmistakable form of Old Jake.

Chapter Ten

A Treasure Found at Home

"Raymie," I said, scarcely able to speak, "There's someone at the door."

"Well, ask 'im in," he said as he came into the room.

I could see he was as taken aback as I was.

We always invited folks in at our house. Mama never even let a drummer stand at the door. She would ask him in, she'd give him a cup of coffee, and sometimes Papa would come up from the shop to join them. Every person at Mama's door was an excuse for a social.

This time Raymie and I forgot our manners and stared back at Mr. Jake, who was staring holes into us.

Then Old Jake said, "I think is all right I come in to talk?"

"Uh, sure, uh, yes, sir, come on in . . ." Raymie said.

I couldn't believe that Raymie had actually asked Old Jake to come into our house, and with the two of us alone!

He walked in, and then I noticed that his hair was combed, and his shirttail was stuck in his pants. I couldn't stop looking at his fingernails. They had been cut. They were a little jagged, but they had been cut right to his fingertips.

He stood there looking from one to the other of us, and then he said, "I come for de tra-sure."

We didn't understand.

"De jewels — de mo-nee."

Raymie was trying not to look scared, but I saw his Adam's apple moving up and down in his throat, the way it did when he was nervous.

"Ohhh . . . yes, sir, Old, I mean, *Mr.* Jake, sir. The fact is, Mr. Jake, there isn't any money, or treasure, or anything. It's just worthless Confederate money. Or did you know that?"

We weren't ready for what happened then. Mr. Jake rushed forward as he made a terrible sound with his throat. Raymie and I grabbed each other. It took us a few moments to realize that he wasn't reaching for us. He was groping for a chair to hold onto. We couldn't believe we were seeing straight, or hearing right. He was crying! His Cajun speech seemed more mixed-up than ever. There was a mixture of French words I had never heard before. It took a while to make any sense out of him at all.

Raymie helped him sit in the chair, and I was amazed to find myself sitting at the feet of this terrible old man who had given me more reason to be afraid in one summer than I had been in all eight others.

His story took a long time, and Raymie and I had a bushel of questions to ask him.

First, he told us how he had lived in Houma, Louisiana, as a boy, and how he had never been farther away from Houma than the places he had gone on shrimp boats in the gulf. When he was forty years old he had an accident on a shrimp trawler. He and the others in the crew were throwing out a "try net" when he slipped and fell. His back had been injured.

"Did you have a wife?" I asked.

This started him crying again, and he told how his wife, Felicité, and their son, had died of a fever after his accident. His coo-zan (cousin) had cared for him many years, but he was a burden to her. Then he had a letter from a man in Bayou La Batre. A relative died and left him a little money, some property, and a house.

"C'est bonne chance! No more make depend on nobody. I come to de Alabama bayou. De mo-nee is enof. No much, mais, enof to live."

"Den, in de house, I find de map. Always, as little boy, I hear about Jean Lafitte — how he come to de bayou countree where I live, many year before I born. How he leave his tra-sures all over de gulf when he live in Barataria, on de Grand Isle. I think, no more I need depend on nobody. I be rich."

"Why did you give us the map?" I asked, scarcely believing I wasn't frightened of him anymore.

94

"When I meet you, I like you. I know you not thieves, that you just coo-rus, like all de 'jeune' people. And I am no strong. I need help to dig."

I looked at Raymie to see if he understood how smart I had been, but he wouldn't look at me.

As I listened, I began to see that we, and the other people in the town, had thought he was odd because we hadn't tried to know him. We had judged him by his speech, his wild hair and eyes.

He laughed when we remembered how fast we had left his house that day.

But his sunken eyes filled with tears again when he told us of the afternoon his house had caught fire. He had overturned grease on his old wood stove, and it had only taken moments for the house to turn into raging flames. There had been time to get a few belongings, the map, and a small amount of money.

"I saw you at the Will-o'-the Wisp." I said.

"In Houma, we say 'Feu Follet.' Yah, I live for while at de ole shack in de marsh, den de people come to see de Feu Follet. I afraid dey find me."

Raymie asked, "Why did you tear off a piece of the map?"

He said that the map seemed to show that the treasure was at Belle's Hammock. When he threw the butcher knife, the corner was torn off. He put the torn piece in his pocket and forgot it. Then, when Hank and Raymie didn't find the treasure at Belle's Hammock, he knew the location must be on that other piece of paper.

And where had he known "Slop Betsy"? He recognized ʌer Cajun accent one day when he heard her at the market. When they talked, it turned out that he had known her husband in Houma. They had shrimped together.

"Maybe you could go back to Houma now," Raymie suggested.

"Me coo-san, she dead," he said, sadly. "I must work. My back, she bad, but I can do for something."

He was living under the old ice plant by the pilings, toward the road, where it is dry. At night he scarcely slept because the mosquitos were so bad.

The strangest thing happened to me then. I felt as if my heart, my mind, every part of me, was going to burst. All the love I had been given by Mama, Papa, Raymie, Jeanne' and other friends, Brother Landry and people at the church, yes, even Hank, swelled up into my throat, which began to ache, and my eyes, which began to spill over. I didn't know where all the tears were coming from.

"Mr. Jake, Sir, don't you worry. Everything's going to be all right. Papa and Mama say all folks are brothers and sisters in God's eyes. They'll figure out a way to help you. If you don't believe it, you can ask Mrs. Potter, who'd be a liar if she didn't agree after the way Mama got rid of the lice for her family. And if she doesn't tell you, you can ask the little Wannamaker kids, the ones whose Papa is always drunk."

"Marcie!" Raymie said. He was mad at me, but I saw tears in his eyes before he ran into the kitchen to get a drink of water.

I heard the car stop out front, and then the gate click, as Mama and Papa came up the walk. I ran out to meet them.

"Mama, Papa! Come in and tell Mr. Jake we'll take care of him. Oh, the *poor man*! He's so nice, Mama, and I'm sorry I said he was a ghost! I should have believed you when you said there weren't such things as ghosts. And Mama - - Papa, maybe he could stay with us? He could sleep in the tool shed. There's the basin and toilet you put in, Papa. The old cot on the back porch would fit in just fine! Oh, please, Mama and Papa, take care of Old Jake like you did the Potters."

As usual, when I was excited, no one understood anything I was saying.

"Marcie!" Mama and Papa both said, in exactly the same way Raymie had said it.

When we walked into the room, Mr. Jake stood up, looking embarrassed.

"What's going on here?!" Papa asked. Too sternly, I thought.

Mr. Jake said he was sorry that he had bothered us, that we were fine children; Papa and Mama must be proud of us. He wouldn't be staying any longer. He had to go home now.

"Papa, he doesn't have a home," I wailed, and that was enough for my pa.

"Where *have* you been living?" he asked. When he heard the answer I thought *he* was going to cry.

That started Old Jake crying again. He said he hadn't cried since his wife and son died twenty-five years ago. He *had* to live under the ice plant. He was a proud man. He had never taken "anything from no one."

I knew Mama had a kind heart and felt bad for Mr. Jake, but you should have seen the horrified look on her face when Papa said, "It wouldn't be *taking*, Mr. Jake. Perhaps you could help me at the shop, and you could help Mrs. Dudley in the yard. With this depression going on I couldn't afford to pay you much, but you could get by just fine here."

I'd seen that look on Mama's face before. The last time was when he Potters came.

Then Papa said, "One sure thing, you're not going anywhere tonight. Mama, why don't you get some sheets and let Marcie make up the cot on the porch? We can talk about fixing up the tool shed tomorrow, Marcie. I reckon we *could* use some more help at the shop, don't you Raymie?"

Raymie grinned and said, "Yes, *sir!*"

Mama and I made the cot, and then Mama dished up some shrimp jambalaya for Mr. Jake and me to eat. We all had dessert together: blanc mange which she had chilled in custard cups on the block of ice in the icebox.

After we finished, Mama said, "Marcie, honey, you've had a long day, and I think you'd better get to bed."

"Yes, ma'am. G'night, Mama. G'night, Papa," I said as I kissed them both.

Raymie dodged and laughed when I came up to him. "Don't kiss me, shrimp," he said,", but then he gave me a soft shove with the palm of his hand. I laughed.

I went to Mr. Jake shyly. "G'night. I hope you're going to stay with us."

"I don' know, little wan," he said, but the smile in his eyes looked like "yes."

In my bedroom I pulled the top sheet down and lay on my back, staring at the ceiling. I wanted him to stay! I could feel that he would. We were going to have wonderful times together. Tomorrow I'd show him the crepe myrtle tree with the moss on it. He'd see how happy we could be, even without Jean Lafitte's treasure.

I was almost asleep when I saw Mama standing in the doorway in her old-fashioned seersucker nightgown. It reminded me of the picture of a missionary lady I had seen, all dressed in white, with a high-necked blouse.

Then the thought came to me, "Mama *is* a missionary. She doesn't want Old Jake to stay here any more than she wanted the Potters. She is willing to do it, though. For Papa, for Raymie and me. Yes, even for Old Jake. If I know Mama, she'll end up doing more for him than any of the rest of us will do, and she'll do it all with love."

Mama's right. I don't have to go to deepest, darkest Africa to be a missionary. I can be one here, like Mama and Papa.

Mama came over and kissed me on the eyelids.

Sleepily, I said, "Mama, I guess I won't go to Africa."

"What?" she asked, in her puzzled-smiling voice.

"Oh, it don't make no difference," I said.

"*Doesn't* make *any,*" Mama said.

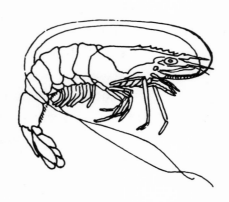

ABOUT THE AUTHOR

Betty Hager was born and raised in Bayou La Batre, Alabama, and took a degree from the University of Alabama where she studied writing under Hudson Strode. She has been a hostess on both railroads and airlines, a high school English teacher, a third grade teacher as well as wife and mother. She is a published children's playwright. Other than writing her interests include little theatre, children's theatre, painting and bridge. She now lives in Southern California.

ABOUT THE ARTIST

Ron Dawkins is a versatile young artist who was born and raised in Las Vegas, Nevada. He has done service in the Merchant Marine and as a medic in the air force. He is an amateur inventor of energy-saving devices, a toymaker and printmaker. He has built his own sailboat and has scratch built automobiles. His current project is to finish a print shop he is constructing from a converted church steeple. It will house his 1890 Chandler and Price press. This is his first book. He lives on the Eastern shore of Mobile Bay with his wife and three children.